The Tale of
Mr. Zebra
and Mrs. Duck

MADELINE MOLINA

PAGE PUBLISHING, INC.
Conneaut Lake, PA

First originally published by Page Publishing 2020

ISBN 978-1-64584-454-9 (pbk)
ISBN 978-1-64584-455-6 (digital)

Printed in the United States of America

This short story is dedicated to my family and friends, especially to Kathy Klipfel for believing in me. Thank you so much for everything. I love you all.

One day on the plains in Africa,
Mr. Zebra was getting a drink,
when something from the sky
fell onto his back and slid down
his face, making him blink.

Mr. Zebra grunted, "OUCH!"
He thought to himself,
"Oh, this is just my luck."
Then he opened his eyes, and
to his surprise, he saw it was Mrs. Duck.

4

Mr. Zebra snorted, "Hello,
are you lost again?
It has been a long time since
I have seen you, my friend."

Mrs. Duck honked back,
"Yes, it has been more than a year.
I have indeed got lost again, I fear."
Mrs. Duck explained she was
flying with the other ducks
when they stopped for some rest.
She was very tired and settled
down on an empty nest.
She thought she must have fallen asleep,
and when she woke up, there was no sound.
Not even a peep.

8

The others had gone and left her alone.

She was very upset and just

wanted to go home.

Mrs. Duck hissed, "I have such a
terrible sense of direction
as you might recall."

Mr. Zebra remembered and snorted,
"It will be okay. You will be
home before fall."

Mr. Zebra, with Mrs. Duck on his back,
trotted briskly away.
Mrs. Duck held on tightly,
trying to not sway.

Mr. Zebra looked back and asked, "Am I going too fast? Are you okay?"

Mrs. Duck quacked, "Oh yes, I am fine. This is turning out to be a lovely day."

Mrs. Duck quacked, "I cannot
thank you enough because I
know this journey is a little rough."

Mr. Zebra snorted, "You are welcome.
It is my pleasure. You can always count
on me to be here for you
because that is what a good friend will do."

21

After traveling a great distance,
they finally arrived near the
outskirts of town.
Mr. Zebra snorted to Mrs. Duck
it was time for her to get down.
Mrs. Duck flew down from Mr. Zebra's back
And quacked, "I remember how to get
home from here. Thank you very much for
the lift, my dear."

Mr. Zebra snorted goodbye as
Mrs. Duck started to cry.
Mr. Zebra said, "Do not cry, my friend.
We will see each other again."
Mrs. Duck quacked back,
"You are right, my dear.
I will come back and
visit you next year."

About the Author

Madeline Molina has been a respiratory therapist for more than twenty-seven years. She enjoys working with adults and children. She loves animals. Her love of animals has inspired many creative stories to keep her children and now grandchildren entertained. She lives close to her family in Oklahoma City, Oklahoma.

CPSIA information can be obtained
at www.ICGtesting.com
Printed in the USA
LVHW070730170620
658107LV00007B/407

9 781645 844549